The Baltimore Years

A collection of poetry and prose

J. Tyler Blue

The Baltimore Years

PretendGeniusPress

London, New York, San Francisco, Seattle, Washington D.C.

All Rights Reserved ©2004 by J. Tyler Blue, Stephen Alexander

No part of this book may be reproduced or transmitted in any form or by any means, graphic, electronic, or mechanical, including photocopying, recording, taping, or by any information storage retrieval system, without the permission in writing from the publisher.

PretendGeniusPress
www.pretendgenius.com

ISBN: 0-9747261-3-3

Printed in the United States of America

"The Most Fantastic Story" previously appeared in Hobart Journal #1 (www.hobartpulp.com)
"My Story" previously appeared at Fictionauts (www.fictionauts.com)
"Morning" previously appeared at Dicey Brown (www.diceybrown.com)
"Charles Street Romance" previously appeared at 3AM Magazine (www.3ammagazine.com)
A shorter version of "Unfinished on the table" previously appeared at Taint Magazine (www.taintmagazine.com)
The following works have appeared at WriteThis Magazine (www.writethis.com) "Kick me, I need some dying" "Masturbating in public" "Baltimore Nights" "Fucking Alice" "Nothing" "My Valentines"

To
Tyus D. and Niko Z.

"Puesto ya el pie en el estribo..."

Inner Harbor

Kick me, I need some dying   1

My Valentines   3

Tuesday perfect   9

Here in Baltimore.   17

My Story   19

Daylight Savings in Baltimore   25

Unfinished on the table   29

Fucking Alice   35

I heard about a coffee shop   39

Masturbating in Public   41

The Most Fantastic Story   43

Hidden   47

Fells Point / Canton

Five Watercolors   53

Morning   57

I speak of Truth and Love   69

Calling the Ex   71

Burning Dear John   73

Gravity   75

To Tyus   77

Vicious Sewing Machine   79

This is the Title   83

here I come   91

Mt Vernon

Because you've seen TV 95

Baltimore Nights 103

Splish Splosh 105

Charles Street Romance 109

boy 115

lover 117

hey love, 119

I started 123

the only one to know 125

Letter dated 03.03.29 129

Forever 133

Nothing 139

Introduction

An explanation of the title of this work provides the best introduction: The Baltimore Years. J. Tyler Blue never uses these words in this particular order in any of his works and indeed some might consider the words pleonastic (whatever that means), but the title hints of Baltimore and of Years. And also of The. In The Baltimore Years we find that Blue brushes the dust from Charm City and immerses himself in it. He never lets the dust settle, however, but freezes it in time around him with haunting and silent prose that allows him to explore his world as a lost astronaut floating amongst the stars might.

> --Sean Brijbasi, Author
> *Still Life in Motion*

Inner Harbor

Kick me, I need some dying

You know I want to talk to you much more than I can. Maybe I want to so much just because I can't. You seem to be willing to follow me into every alley I run down. Perhaps you are just amused. I would be too I guess.

Sometimes I want to be punched in the face so hard my lower lip bleeds. I need to feel that sting and understand that swell to get closer. Closer to being me.

My kite string is running out just as the wind is picking up. Tennessee never looked so far away.

I bet your eyes are stunning when you stand out on the back porch at night right where the light from the kitchen window begins to fade and the cricket noise starts to become a mournful cry for friendship.

I yell, I scream, I sulk, I whisper, I do what I can to have you see my shadow more than my skin.

Are your nails red? Are they long enough to draw blood on my back if I pin you down and bite your neck?

I need your understanding more than your treasure. But I will settle if you don't have any more tea to share.

There are pauses in my thinking. This isn't a sign of my weakness, only a prelude.

I want us to converse through dreams, like they do in the movies.

I can't seem real to you, by being real to myself. What is missing from me can be found in you, but it isn't a key, only a nice tight fit, until the friction wears away the edges and we fall into memory...

Come to Baltimore.

My Valentines

It was another God damn Valentines night alone. It seemed like every single person I knew was with someone, making them of course, not single. So you know, I thought it would be a great idea to go to this Howard Dean convention. I am not a supporter really but I thought who else could be as heart broken and desperate than Dean supporters right now?

So I went down there, 203rd Davis Street at the old Otto Bar. Not far from the Inner Harbor where all the stupid tourist go. That is where I should have went, maybe I could catch some couple in a fight, console some girl. Take her back to my place and fuck the shit out of her, or even better yet in the Hyatt or whatever hotel she could be staying at. That would have been a sweet night.

But no, I go to the old Otto Bar. I walk in and not much has changed except all the decorations which I guess means the walls are still in the same place but everything is new inside but it doesn't really feel new. They have this old monkey stuffed and behind the bar, actually they have several monkeys stuffed and behind the bar. The place looks run down and too far north, I look out the window to make sure I'm still in Baltimore and not Biloxi. I guess I got there kind of early, it seems like I always get to places kind of early. I ordered some Makers Mark. A double, no rocks. After some time the place starts to fill up and I have one of those meaningless conversations with the bar tender. Rick, Rick the bar tender. Anyway soon enough some dude gets up on the small stage.

"Hey. Um. Well, Happy Valentines everyone. And uh, thanks for coming out."

The mostly college kid crowd gives a good response. Something typical, something ordinary and I don't look up while he continues to talk. I light another cigarette and stare at one of the monkeys. I wonder if he ever had a name.

The Dean organizer guy at the mic goes on and on about continuing the fight and I start looking around to see what kind of strange I can maybe end up with tonight. I remember what happens next like it was clearly the worst thing to ever happen to me. I mean ever.

His name was Anthony; I remember that clearly because I always wanted my name to be Anthony. He was a good looking guy, a little taller than me which is to say maybe six foot one and he looked like he played lacrosse or soccer or something. Thin but in shape. Anyway him and his two buddies, I don't remember their names and I don't really care to either, they start talking to me. They each bum a cig. I light them up and Anthony smiles. With a God damn cigarette in his mouth he asks me if I smoke. I inhale on my cig.

"I don't have any."

"Well, we do. You want some?"

Sure, what the fuck, I had nothing else going on. Why not I thought to myself. Why the fuck not. So we go outside around the corner to an alley. I take some monster hits off Anthony's pipe he calls Morrison. Now, I've smoked before but I am not a professional and I wasn't paying much attention to shit. I was just taking big hits and getting fucked up.

Fucked up is right. The world slowed the fuck down and it seemed like my head was getting reset every thirty seconds. Maybe less. I don't know. It seemed to take years to walk back into the bar and people were talking but I couldn't care less about what they were saying because I had no idea what the fuck they were talking about. It was some strange world of being too high yet still aware of shit. I knew where I was, I knew what I was doing there but I didn't know how long I had been standing in one place. Anthony said something to me about going to the bathroom. His friend nodded his head as if I should follow so I did. Why? Because I couldn't think of anything else to do and I was fucked up.

So we go upstairs and all four of us fill in to the bathroom. I'm thinking were going to take some more hits but I'm way too gone for any of that. Anthony unzips his pants and looks at me.

"Suck my cock."

I laugh and say no thanks. But no one else thinks its funny and suddenly I'm trying to come down out of the clouds.

"Do it for the Dean campaign."

"Fuck Dean." Is all I can remember saying right then. One of them, the one that looks like he is Greek or Jewish or something I don't know. Fucking Hamas or some shit punches me dead in the face. I am kicked and all sorts of shit and being so fucking high I think the pauses between blows are minutes so this beating felt like days. I don't know, shit, or I just don't want to get into it but a cock went into my ass. Thrust after thrust and I started laughing. Another punch to my face stopped that. They fucked me, each of them and I just moaned. They were grabbing my hips and pulling me back and I could feel their balls smacking up against me. One of them cum'd on my back another on the back of my head and I think one of them cum'd in my ass.

They left me there on the floor with my pants down around my ankles and my lip bleeding my eye fucking swollen. With cum on my back, my ass, and my God damn head for Christ sake. And I puked. All over the floor, my hands, my shirt. I stumbled around and got dressed. Splashed water on myself and lit a fucking cigarette.

I made my way downstairs, paid my tab and left. I took a cab home, he asked me what happened and I just said "Valentines happened."

I walked up to my apartment and fell down on the steps. I fucking cried until I passed out and my neighbor woke me up on Sunday morning.

She asked if I was alright and I said yeah. Just fine.

"Just had a tough Valentines, that's all."

Embarrassed I fumbled for my keys and dropped them. She picked them up and opened my door. I didn't even look at her. I said thanks, and she held my hand.

"Hey, you alright?"

"Yeah, I just uh, had a rough night."

"Well, if you want to talk you can just come over."

I smiled and looked at her. Where was she yesterday? I closed the door behind me. Took off my clothes and cried. Happy Valentines. Happy fucking Valentines.

Tuesday perfect

There was nothing perfect about what I did. Nothing perfect about me at all. But at the time, well, at the time that wasn't true. I was perfect, and I knew it.

You see this starts as most good true love stories start. We saw each other and promptly and correctly ignored each other. It was at the doctor's office. I remember it was a Tuesday. Tuesday afternoon in fact. I noticed her and her short blonde hair, and little hair clips. Very stylish. Very pneumatic and stylish.

We saw each other around campus. Ended up having a class together. She may have been interested in me by then. I don't know. I only know I couldn't look at her. I couldn't for fear of being caught staring. She always had clips in her hair. I didn't look long. I really didn't. I was, you understand, busy doing schoolwork on whatnot. I was also extremely busy on the weekends in those days. Very busy thinking of all the things I might do. Twenty-seven tiles across and eighteen down.

I went out one night with a group of friends. We met up by what we called a smoke shack, or smoke pit near one of the dorms. She was there. A guy was talking to her, telling her that she looked good in her "go get 'em skirt." She laughed and leaned back. I remember thinking how pneumatic she was and what a pig he was for saying that to her. She looked at me. Of course I looked away. It isn't polite to stare. That is why I looked away of course.

"Wow Jack. I didn't think you would be here!"
She knew my name. I smiled compulsively. But I assure you; it was not some Jerry Lewis smile. Please give me some credit here. I stood, back straight as mother taught me and smiled.

"Oh? Why not?"

"You just don't seem like the type."

"Oh, I'm the type."

Indeed I am. I am quite the type you see. I go out all the time. Just not with her, or these people. Of course I said that not so matter of fact, more jovial.

I was in that kind of mood. My friends laughed. They too were in a jovial mood.

We went to a club in town. We drank illegally and danced like criminals. Lord, she was a good dancer. I didn't dance so much. I wasn't from this town and wanted to first see what style was popular in the local area before applying my self. You understand. She however, seemed to fit right in. She also it seemed, had a boyfriend.

A tall young man who also liked to dance. However, I may add he didn't seem to be so good at it. He mostly stood there and admired her dancing next to him. He would also rudely place his hands on her hips and other places. She didn't seem to mind so much, but she probably for some reason, has never been treated with great dignity that she deserves. I would need to save her. I would need to treat her justly.

She started to talk to me in class after that night. About school work mostly. Then sometimes about this or that. I wanted to ask her out, but I was conflicted you see. She had a boyfriend, and I certainly didn't want to disrupt such a thing. Not to mention at this time I was having a particular rough time with acne.

She was late to class a few times. She explained to me that she was sleeping at a friend's dorm room. Doug, she mentioned.

"A friend of Mike's?"

"Who?"

"Your boyfriend."

"Oh, no. We are kind of not seeing each other anymore."

She was drinking and Doug let her sleep over. She explained they "don't really go out, but hang out from time to time."

She was lost. I needed to save her. To stop her from being used as meat. I started to see how the men on campus viewed her. Her tight pants and half shirts. So beautiful. So lost. I needed to show her that she is worthy of so much more.

We started talking so much more. We even had dinner a few times. I admitted to her that I was a virgin. She smiled. She was so beautiful.

"I had sex with a virgin before."

"Oh?"

"Actually twice before."

"Ah"

"They were not any good. I said to myself 'Jessica, don't ever have sex with a virgin again.' And I haven't."

"Well you don't have to worry about me. I won't have sex with you."

"No kidding. You're a virgin. Anyway, I am not interested."

We kept talking from time to time. I resigned myself to only being a friend. This was more than enough really. In this role I can help her see herself as a beautiful woman who doesn't need to sleep around for respect.

One night we kissed. It was unlike anything I ever felt. I felt as if I was swimming in color. She too felt something. She expressed that I was unlike any other man she ever met. Yes, I was unlike any other man she ever met. I had true emotional feelings.

I proclaimed my love for her that very evening. She said she loved me and we kissed more violently and passionately than before. We parted that night, happy and in love.

A few days later she was late to class. Greg's room.

"I couldn't tell him no."

"Why?"

"Because I just couldn't. Listen, we'll talk tonight. Meet me at my dorm room."

I did so. I brought flowers. She cried and told me she was sorry. We were not dating anyway I said. It is okay. I am so big. So big.

I went home and cried that night and swore I would never see her again outside of class. But you understand, I was in love. We saw each other, kissed and talked about life and everything. She said to me that she only wanted me.

"Even though I am a virgin."

She laughed and kissed me so hard I nearly fell over. We laughed together.

February seventh, a Saturday. I remember it was raining and cold. We were in her room. For the first time in my life I made love. She was beautiful. Every bit as I imagined. Every bit.

I was more than swimming in color. I was the king of purple and the prince of red. I was so sparkling in my own image; I was divine. We were together and all was in order with the world.

We spent the entire weekend together. Heaven was a dorm room. She was mine, and I was hers. Nothing was greater than we were. Perfection incarnate.

Tuesday she was late to class and my crown fell.

Perfect. Tuesday perfect.

Here in Baltimore.

There is nothing clever with being clever anymore. There is nothing special about being alone or even admitting to having a small penis. Nobody is ever really impressed by such honesty these days.

No today is about being refreshingly idealistic. Cryptic and hopeful. Happy in a melancholy sort of way. Let's all hold hands and pretend we understand the 60's so much we might as well have been there.

Place picture magnets of me on your fridge. I'm not afraid of frames anymore.

Let's be bold this time and stop saying what we really want other people to hear. Let's just be what they want us to be. Sexy. Free. Magical. Potent. The stuff dreams are made of.

I miss the whisperings in my ear. Such admissions are frowned upon I know. You have a life. I have my crayons.

Stars seem less bright as I get older. The paper a little rougher. I am wrong for mentioning such things. There is nothing new in what I say. I am not sure there ever was.

I love you

I know about the sunflowers. I know about the color yellow. I know it doesn't matter when I tell you these things. It doesn't hurt me either. I'm beautiful like that.

My Story

He is a young six-year-old boy. I don't see him often but when I do he is always full of joy. A kind of joy that is contagious. I have seen him make strangers smile. He is my son and I think of him. I would tell you how often but you wouldn't believe me so let it be understood that I think of him. I want you to know that. It is important that you know, that he knows.

My lawyer says it is a good idea that I write this down. That it might be helpful for my time in court. Of course I'll get to more of that later. But I want to make it clear before we really begin that I am not writing this for my lawyer, for me or for this trial. I am writing this for him. And for you too I guess. I want you to know my story and I want you to make sure he knows my story. Since this has happened I've really begun to understand what is important in this world and what really is not. This here, this is important.

About four months ago I took a friend to a downtown clinic. This clinic does work for free, like mammograms, pregnancy tests and consultations and they also test for HIV. They do this work for people, like my friend who really can't afford it otherwise. Chris is scared of needles and well, he's scared to find out if he has HIV or not. So I took him to the clinic. To be there for him. And to take the test with him.

We got our results a day apart. Chris called me after work on a Thursday. I remember because Maryland was playing Duke that night. He was happy and he was going to get drunk. I remembered we laughed. "All that stress for what?" I said.

I got a phone call the very next day. It was the clinic. I tested positive. For HIV.

I can't begin to tell you what that day or many days after that was like because beyond those facts I can't remember a damn thing. I can't remember going back to the clinic. I can't remember them telling me to remain calm but I'm sure they did. They said a different Lab would perform the test. I would only have to wait 72 hours. Then if need be there is still yet another lab in Los Angeles that can run a test. It happens, they said, that sometimes there are false readings.

Positive. Positive. And positive. Where was I? What the hell was I doing?

I quit my job. I was crazy. I smoked as much weed as I could fucking get and I drank myself out of every bar in Fells Point, Canton, and Federal Hill. Friends and drugs kept me afloat. I don't remember much beyond these facts. I don't know where I was or why or how or anything really. I was in a trance or something for weeks upon weeks.

I don't know what I was doing on Baltimore Street. I mean I was getting drunk, getting high, getting lost. I didn't ask for her to come up to me. I didn't ask her to talk to me. I didn't think to ask her much of anything. And she didn't either. I mean this is a two-person thing isn't it?

But yeah I remember some things. The way she leaned forward on her toes when I bit her ear lobe. The way her ass felt good in my hands. The way it felt to be inside her. The way it felt to forget things and be normal. Be fucking normal and alive.

I'm no killer it just sort of ended up that way. Lisa in the fucking anti-miracle of anti-miracles got HIV. I don't know what to say. I'm sick. I mean I feel sick over this whole thing. I don't know what to do.

So I'm on trial and I'm dying faster everyday. I never meant to hurt anybody, I just didn't want to hurt anymore. I just didn't think it all out. But now I think every day. All the damn time, I think.

I think of my son. I think of where I fucked up. I could have lived this out. I could have maybe got that cure that they are talking about now. I could have done a lot of things. I could have been a father.

My God, I'm sorry.

I love you Ty and I'm sorry. Daddy is sorry. I'm so sorry. I messed up. Don't be like me.

So there. There it is. My story. My human story, don't forget that part. I'm human. So yeah, I made mistakes that maybe you wouldn't but I'm no less human. I am just a man. So please take something good from this and make sure my son hears it. I want him to be a man too.

Just a better one than me.

Daylight Savings in Baltimore

I

I will speak to you as though you are me. We will share blood and electrons. We will pretend to understand. Maybe even believe.

II

I went to the library to drop off a book that was overdue. I saw woman in a red shirt and blue jeans. A white sweater was wrapped around her waist. Her blonde hair was up and I could imagine.

III

I went to the movies alone. The soda/popcorn combo was more than the movie ticket. I finished the movie and rushed to the bathroom. I left my soda unfinished in protest of its largeness. Also, I was already bloated.

IV

I was standing in Barnes and Noble reading from a book I had brought with me. It is a book on "mathimatical perspectives on our chaotic Constitution." I was standing in the Business section when I laughed softly to myself. I looked up and saw her walking away. But he was looking right at me.

V

I wore a green t-shirt today. I haven't shaved since Thursday. The sun felt good on my skin.

VI

"Okay can I go now?"
(pause)
Sure Ty.
"Which button to hang up?"
I don't know...
The red one she says

VII

She looked in my direction. I smiled quickly but was too shy to continue eye contact. She kept walking with her cart full of books. "Employees Only." The sign was white with black letters and had a small crack in the lower left corner. I didn't stare long.

VIII

Driving with my window down my shaved head felt cold. I remember making a photo copy of my left hand and writing a small poem on the palm. I folded it carefully before sending it in the mail. It wasn't a day like this. Maybe I should wear a hat.

IX

On my way in to Wal-Mart I was thinking of wit. My use of it and your use of it. Maybe it is a lie. A form of deception. I am scared you see. I use wit to deceive. To hide the truth from me and you. I think maybe you do the same. It is not so funny anymore. Why am I here anyway?

X

Today is daylight savings. I have either lost an hour or spent one less hour alone. I cannot decide which is more pathetic.

XI

It is another ordinary day in Baltimore.
It is another day gone in Baltimore.
It is Baltimore.
And it is me.

Unfinished on the table

"I left my story unfinished on the table. I say unfinished to everyone I talk to. The truth is, I left it unwritten. But this is a matter of words and writers like myself are not interested in small matters words. We are champions of ideas, movements and ages. If you can't understand this, then I suggest you find another unfinished story to read."

She stares at me and I am not sure if she can blink. I began to wonder if she could blink. Maybe she was missing her eyelids. Her eyeliner placement was impeccable and impressive. However, I didn't get to wonder long about her eyelids, her voice indicated the answer plainly. "What?"

"Yes." What more do I need to say? This must be some sort of joke.

"I mean, what do you mean? How can I read it if you didn't even write it?"

"Oh, don't bother me with who wrote my story. But certainly if you must know I didn't write it at all. I have mentioned this to you already. Do you blink?"

"What is that? A drug reference?" Now she brightened. Leaned backward and not forward like I had thought she would. Maybe she was indicating something to me. Something I had not yet thought of. Drugs?

"Drug reference?" I should not have said that. Now she would have the power. I thought you were not supposed to wear white until after Memorial Day. I am not certain, perhaps I should divorce this thought quickly before I create a scandal.

"You are a strange man. Do you know that? My friend was so certain I would like you." Her voice trailed off at that point and while I am normally very interested in speaking about me, the waiter and his crotch were distracting.

"Your martini, sir. And your vodka tonic…" Another voice trailing off.

I imagine he was staring at her and she at him. I say imagine because I couldn't help but look at his penis that was a mere six inches away from my nose. Did he have to stand so close? With his bare penis that close to my mouth? It wasn't really bare of course, but what are a few threads? I will tell you, after three martinis a few articles of clothing are nothing. Nothing at all.

"So, how do you know Kelly?" Her lips were fuller than they were earlier. I figured that it must be the vodka, the waiter or my cologne that is doing this to her. I must find out.

"We had phone sex." Coup de grace. I now had control again and calmly drank my fourth martini.

"What?" She blurted this out with some laughter mixed in. I know several tables looked at us. If she was not careful I would mention Memorial Day. It would not be pretty, I let my eyelids do the talking while I did the speaking. The message should be clear enough now.

"Yes. In the rain no less."

"In the rain? How does one have phone sex in the rain?" She asked as if I was lying. What a foolish woman.

"One doesn't have phone sex. Two people have to be involved. Unless it is a phorgy then it is more of course. But I haven't done that since college."

Just then a woman wearing a white blouse walked by casually. Perhaps I am wrong about the dates and colors or perhaps this place is more lewd than I had thought. She noticed the woman too.

"I am afraid to ask…"

"I am too." We made a connection. We both smile with our excitement at such rebelliousness. It is great to be alive. I picked up one of the three empty martini glasses and stare through it.

"Did you hear of the new art exhibit?" I ask. Art is a new word for chaos.

"With the blood?" She asked but she knew the answer. I hate that.

"Do you play backgammon?"

"Of course. But you knew that." She smiled at me and she knew what was coming. God, I hate that too.

"I will beat you tonight." She moaned ever so slightly. I barely heard it myself.

"I was told you were a good player." She spoke more as her fingers glided over my passion and inserting themselves in key locations to keep me focused. Obviously she is a player too.

I clenched the sheet on the table tightly and bit my bottom lip. It was all I could do to contain myself. So much depends on my question "Do you want to go first?"

Fucking Alice

I got a gun. It ain't real but that don't matter. Nobody really know the difference anyways when I stick it up in they face. Like I did to this girl last night. All she did is scream. And yell and flop around and all this other crazy shit. She kept on saying her damn name to me like that would not make me want to fuck her. Or maybe she was trying to get me to fuck her. I ain't never fucked no Alice before. But really alls I wanted was some damn money.

See people like me we need what people like her got. Money. And nice shoes. And good clothes. And watches. Yeah, we need watches so we know what time these fools be getting off ov work so we can go rob they asses. I treat 'em like customers really. I say "Hey, welcome to my street. Now give me yur money bitch-ass!" And then I show 'em the gun. It's a damn good gun. Until Alice, that crazed bitch, broke that shit.

I went up to her all gentlemen like 'cause I know how these bitches are. All playa hatin' on anybody from the streets at first but after you gets to know 'em all they want is a little thug in 'em. So I goes up to her and say "Scuse me lady, you got a light?" Then I stood there all Clark Gable like but more modern, more P Diddy but a little more rugged. I had that smooth but hard look going. I had that shit down. I had it good cause as soon as I said it she damn near broke her leg trying to stop. She's all "Oh, I don't smoke." and all that shit but I wasn't gonna let this shit get away, you know what I'm sayin'?

So I start kicking my game and she was all eatin' it up like she was starving. She was straight up starving for some gangsta shit up in her. Man she was straight diggin' my shit. I was 'bout to just straight kick it with her, maybe go back to her place and hit it some but I had other shit to do that night. So I start walking her down this alley where I do my business you know. Not out where the po po can come and snatch me or some other damn fool and come try to be Superdude or whatever. I ain't no fighter. I ain't trying to get all up and sweaty and breakin' bones and that shit.

Man I could prolly kill somebody if I throw a punch with all my might. I seriously hurt 'em. Damn fools, running up on me.

Anyway, I took her back in that alley, gave her my line. My line that I done put a paten on it. "Hey, welcome to my street. Now give me yur money bitch-ass!" It's all about delivery. It's all about timing and shit. Right when I say money that's when I break out the gun and I kind ov really give it to 'em on 'bitch-ass' for that added extra dimension ov effect. You know.

So I said that shit and she went up and started actin' a fool. Screaming her name "Oh I'm Alice, I'm Alice, Oh, Oh my god." And all that shit. Looking damn stupid. I was 'bout to shoot her ass but my gun didn't have any bullets in it. It was fake. So I just yelled at her. "Shut the fuck up Alice! Before I shoot yur ass!"

She did. Then I thought damn. I got mad game. I could probably make her suck my dick right now. She probably wanted to. The way she was eyeing me up and shit. She probably wanted to lick my asshole or some other kind ov freaky shit. Fucking freak. I was about to let her go right then because I was just like "Damn, why don't I just do what she wants me to do and then rob her ass." But then she just went off again. She looked like Jackie Chan but like a more bitch version ov it. All this monkey jumping and shit acting all crazed. I was like damn these rich girls got crazy ways ov wanting to sex people up! But she kicked the shit out ov my hand and broke my damn gun.

"My name is Alice!"

That scared the shit out ov me. Who the fuck got to be yellin' yur own name? I picked up the piece ov my gun and ran. I ain't scared to tell you that. This bitch is crazed. I ain't never fucking with no Alice again. Never.

Broke my damn gun. I really should ov punched her. But that ain't my style.

But damn.

Fucking Alice broke my damn gun.

I heard about a coffee shop

I need a coffee shop like that.
I need to leave this apartment.
I need something.
Perhaps a cup of coffee in my hand
one that could carry my right hand as much
but I feel patient and I am insubstantial and in the
necessity of a coffee shop.
And the friends or the steam of
oh, of the breathing...

I am pleasant.
Think! the red newspaper and the nails.
My new smile and I will fall as yesterday,
secret and wrinkled on the floor.

I will pretend to look for sugar or a spoon.
It would be perhaps
(and she would be)
pleasantly true.

Masturbating in Public

I am reading Milton
in the bath,
in the subway,
in between looks
at a young college student with perky breasts,
and daytrips to the beach

I am letting Milton play
in the 21st Century
mind of mine, I am hearing him in a Wolf Blitzer
way explain the political crisis of the Angels.
Could this be made into a movie? Hugh Grant
might have a role,
yes I think Stephen Spielberg would direct.

I am reading Milton
to include him on my list.
"Calvin Klein
has got a new underwear ad."
I heard her say to her boyfriend
or was he just a friend, a coworker perhaps

I go to chat rooms to explore
possible meanings behind Milton's words

such discussions range from lunch menus to playful cyber sex.
"Who is Beelzebub?" I say
"Who is who?" "What is that?" "A/S/L?"
I met a girl who looks nice from Oklahoma
and another from just outside London

Perhaps I will meet them
when I am done with Milton
we'll sit around
and talk about "South Park"
the pandemonium of terror
and David Beckham.

The Most Fantastic Story

The building did not look impressive in the morning sunlight. It never does. The people leaving the building looked equally unimpressive. All nameless entities going to nameless jobs in other unimpressive buildings in other parts of the Grand City.

It was a grand city. Mostly because of how many unimpressive buildings were in it. The size of the building didn't matter. The larger the building the less it was noticed. The smaller the building and the people were more likely to forget it was there. That happened from time to time.

The Grand City had many unimportant things going on. The most unimportant one was the creation of the most fantastic story ever created. This is unimportant because nobody reads stories anymore. They only hear about them. Like one would hear about so and so that once dined at such and such a place for some occasion or another some time ago. All very unimportant when matched against the immensity of everything.

The most fantastic story ever created had everything one would ever want in a story. It really had it all. It was so fantastic that as soon as it was published everybody started to talk about it. Nobody read it of course but everybody talked about it.

What the poor people liked the best was the way the characters were so deftly created. They really got into talking about that.

The semi educated loved to discuss the plot. How it climbed and climbed until the perfect moment for a climax. Yes, it was something to say about that.

The educated were really enthralled with the symbolism of it all. How such and such character was really representing the common man and the objects like the clock or the birds meant time or death or something like that. There was quite a bit of debate and vigorous discussion about it all.

Of course even the anti-social had something to say about it. How it was too commercial and how the author who once wrote a lesser book, but one that was once more accessible by being so obscure sold out to make it big. Many things were said about this selling out.

The author even had things to say. Mostly he said he didn't want to say anything. Occasionally he talked, but he liked to discuss the weather. "Rain makes you wet you know." That was his favorite saying. He said it all the time.

He jumped off the roof of an unimpressive building this morning and made quite a mess on the street. Nobody was overly impressed or awed by it. His head was flat from the impact. His leg still twitched for a few moments. He was wearing yellow shoes.

Hidden

There is this happening and that happening
and little kids having sex in back of churches
and old people eating ice cream on swing sets.

In between it all buildings are falling and hearts
are being broken
and pieces are being lost
and a wedding cake is being spoiled by the sun.
or the rain.
or whatever it is that might spoil it.

Here and there you sit
you stand
you do things
and I do things
and we do things
that have nothing to do with what I say
or what you think or what she is or how he was.

Things just go on.

Somewhere here or there
I bled and you cried
or I cried and someone's mom was shot

and you screamed and I didn't hear it
or I felt bad because
I have my reasons
and you cut something with a knife
or a word
or maybe both.

So it goes that you are saying things and I am doing things
that aren't having anything to do with each other
but are related in the time it takes for a car to crash into my sunshine
and bring me more of what I already think I have enough of
but that isn't the point of me
nor is it the point of you
nor him, nor her, nor anyone really.

I can't sing the blues anymore
because you don't share the sheets at night in Toronto
and my feet are cold in Baltimore.

When I saw there were no strings to cut
my heart sank
and I knew I would have to find something else to fill my time.

What I really mean to say here is being criminal is
a way.

Cool, rage, smoking, breaking, smite, cool, fucking
cool,
so cool it hurts to be so damn cool
but I still come up empty in my mind
when I add up all the things I think and see
and was and believe.

Can you understand?

Can I understand?

Does it matter if I did,
or if you did, or if he did, or if she did,
we can't trade skin,
so "fuck off and leave me alone" a little girl said

Princess.
Princess - don't call me that mom!
I have a heart and a dream.
they don't go together but damn it all I am here to
be served.
I want to be in the green,
I want to be in the cream,
I want to be, just be, just be, just be.

I had plans.
they were small but pointless.
I scribbled on a wall.
I found a toy Jesus in a sewer
and he said that is where he belonged.

Not him, not her, not you.
but me.

It isn't need but hope that kills.
I hope you hear me.
I hope you understand.
I hope you do okay.
I hope I don't care.
I hope I don't care.
I hope I don't care.

(hush)

Fells Point / Canton

Five Watercolors

Plausability

I know several women who seem to have little problem sleeping around. My mother is one of these women, so when I say sleep around I don't mean it in some way you might expect. I say it only as a matter of fact. A fact that is proven time and time again over the course of say, a few weeks or months. So, what does it mean that I state it at all?

Well, I wanted to make a clear distinction between them and myself. I suppose it is better if I start out with comparing other men to myself. I know some men who seem to have little problem sleeping around. What is the difference between myself and these men and these women, my mother included? I have several theories on the matter.

Adaptability

There is a boy who lives across the street from me. He is from Mexico and is very good with his feet. I know because from my window I have seen him run up and down a nearby alley kicking a ball.

A few days ago I saw his older sister drawing lines on the sidewalk. Her dress was pink and she wore white socks. Was she crying? I couldn't tell from this angle. I closed my window blinds and whistled something I thought sounded Japanese.
I never did see the boy again.

Scalability

I am ugly. And despite being listed as one of Baltimore's most available bachelors I am still ugly.

My best remedy for this problem is to stand in the rain with no overcoat. Sure this is dangerous, but I am a desperate man. You cannot understand the reasons of an ugly man so I will not attempt to explain them. You are beautiful. I know because my words speak only to beautiful people. It is a curse in some ways that I can find you in this way but were we to meet you would be disgusted and call me names so filthy and horrible I cannot bear to say them here.

It has rained often as of late but the sun is the monster eye and it will discover me again. I hold the jagged edge of a broken wine bottle.

Implacability

I was shopping for food not long ago at my local grocery store. I turned down the cereal isle and saw an older woman smoking. She stood there smoking her cigarette and comparing the fat calories of three popular cereal brands. I approached her and asked what she was doing smoking in the store.

I never asked for her name and she never gave it. I never gave mine either so it is conceivable that we never met.

I bought oatmeal and pears. I believe the pears are now rotting in some trash heap.

Corrigibility

Most of my day and night I spend at home. My phone never rings yet I own an answering machine. I have three unplayed messages on the machine. They have been that way for months. I think since shortly after I moved in to this apartment. I don't know how to play them so they have just been sitting there making the little light on the machine blink over and over again.

I think of how much we have in common and it is good that we have each other. I can't say that about any other machine in my apartment. Or for that matter any other object at all. I do have a painting, but I don't really connect to it anymore.

I used to I guess. It is a painting of the sun illuminating a sunflower in one view and on the other of a sunflower illuminating the sun. I painted it using five watercolors.

I felt the warmth of the night air last night. I thought about walking and narcissistic numbers, over and over again, but I never felt like a lion. Then I thought, "the refrigerator light!" And slept.

Morning

There were birds chirping. I did not hear them. I have heard them before. On a Monday, I think. Today is not Monday. But I am sure they were chirping.

I went into the city. Nobody was talking about birds chirping. I asked around. No one could say for certain that they heard the birds this morning. But they all were sure that the birds were chirping. Even if it isn't Monday.

I sat down on a bench next to the street to have a smoke. Cheap cigarettes never do it right. I have to smoke two to make up for it, but then they lose the appeal of being cheap.

Leala doesn't understand. How can she? She is a woman.

I went to work. But it was unimportant. So I will not talk about it. After leaving work I sat on the bench next to the street to have a smoke.

"Hello Ben."

I nodded. That is what people do when they are busy, or not wanting to say anything. I wasn't either of those things. But I like to pretend that I have a great many things on my mind. In fact I was only thinking about the chirping. Or lack of really.

He sat down next to me. He has a name but I have forgotten it. I talk to him sometimes. He does not have cheap cigarettes. Of course you can tell right off by looking at his shoes that he would not ever smoke cheap cigarettes. This is a man I really should get to know. I know that I should.

"How's it going ol' chap" I say. I tried smiling. I know that people like it when you smile.

He was inhaling right then when I said that. So he did not respond right away. He looked off for a moment. Like he saw a bird. I looked in that direction and did not see one.

Perhaps I just missed it.

"Quite well Ben. Quite well." He said that as he rubbed his hand down the thigh of his pants. Not in a gay way, but in a way that people do when they have nothing else to do with their hands. His pants looked liked they felt nice anyway. I would probably rub my hands on my pants all the time if I were wearing pants like those. As it was, I only rub my hair. What is left of it anyway.

"What are your plans this weekend?"

I blinked. Blink. Blink. I have no plans but you do not say that to a man like this. Not if you want to get to know him.

"Well uh, ya know. Maybe watch a little football. Drink a few cold ones. Uh, maybe later go out with the Misses or something. You know." I nod. With authority to send the message with my body as well as my language. These things are noticed by the subconscious mind.

"Yes. Yes." The second "yes" seemed to fall out of him as he again starred off in some direction taking in the smoke. He turned his head to me. His eyes are quite beautiful. I don't say that in a way that you might think. I think it is fine for one man to think another to have beautiful eyes.

"Why don't you come to my party on Saturday?" He smiled. I guess I am like other people. I felt more at ease when he smiled.

"I'll have to confer with the Misses. You understand." I gave one of those laughs. Those you understand laughs. He laughed a bit too. As if to say he understood. Which I think he did.

"Of course. Well, let me give you my address. I do hope you come." He gave me the paper with his address. His penmanship wasn't sharp, but it was clear enough. I've never been to Canton. I wondered if he heard the birds chirping this morning.

He left before I could ask. I had another smoke because my cigarettes are cheap and because I felt accomplished. I was social climbing.

I did not go to the party. I cannot truly remember why, but I know that we did not go. Leala was being a pain in my ass as women can be. More over I just don't think when Saturday evening came around I was up to driving to Hamden. I felt it would be a long drive and I just wasn't up for it right then.

It must have been Tuesday afternoon, after work when I was having my smoke when I saw him again.

"I missed you Saturday." Suddenly I felt very low for not going. I took a heavy drag and held it for a moment. I nodded and mentioned something about being busy. What I said I can't truly remember nor is it that important really.

"Well, you should have come. There was plenty of food and drink."

I nodded taking another drag.

"Even sex."

He didn't say it so far apart to increase emphasis. But there was a pause as he let it slip out like it was normal fare. I tried not to look in his direction for a moment. I stared at the nothing cars with the nothing people in them driving to nothing places.

"Sex?" I inhaled. Not too deeply. Body language you know.

"Mmm" He hummed but not really hummed. It was what people say yes to when they are too tired to say yes or when it is of course obvious that the answer is yes. He did not seem tired. His flicked his ashes. I watched them fall to the concrete. He rubbed his pant leg.

"Well, I think in a few weeks I might have another one. Perhaps you will be less busy."

"Yeah. Leala is thinking of seeing her cousin anyway. Maybe I will have an easier time escaping." I gave a short laugh.

"Oh please bring her." His hand now resting on my shoulder squeezed. Not hard nor too soft to be like a woman. But how a man does to another man. I understood.

"I would very much like it for both of you to come." He smiled. He had quite a lovely smile.

Things happened in-between that time and the party. But they were boring and I can't remember it all anyway. I think however, on one of those days I did hear birds chirping. But I might be wrong. Actually the more I think about it; the more I am sure I did not hear any birds chirping. No one seems to be very concerned about it though.

We showed up at the party. I told Leala it was better to be late. So we showed up at 7:05. Five minutes I think is good. Not too late really but late.

The door was opened but it wasn't him. It was someone else. It didn't matter, we were let in. There weren't many people there when we showed up. I got drinks for us. We socialized for sometime. More and more people showed up. But it never felt overly crowded.

"BEN!" He was spirited. His cheeks a bit red. Or perhaps I imagined that because I imagine your cheeks are supposed to be red when you are feeling spirited.

"This is Leala." I was introducing them. But he cut me off. Not in a rude way, but in a very stylish way.

"Leala, what a lovely name. I am Richard. Are you finding things okay?" His smile was especially bright. I don't believe he ever had a cavity. It is quite a thing to have a cavity you know. Quite a thing.

"Ben, do you like boats?" He went on to introduce me to a friend of his who has a boat. A boat that was in fact just down on the water not far from the house. Leala stayed with Richard as I went to the boat.

I remember a few of us going on a bit of a ride. It was fun with the wind in our hair. Soon it became dark and we docked. But not at Richards house. It was another house that was having a party. I did not know anyone there but soon it did not matter. We were all merry and filled with drink and smoke. It must have been hours I cannot truly remember.

Sometime late or early as it was a woman and I were kissing. Who she was I cannot really remember. It was as it sometimes is with drinks and smokes. She tossed her hair over her shoulders in that way that invites. I felt comfortable in my shoes but shifted my weight in a way to move forward without moving at all. Soon it became my intent to have her. And it was easy to tell she wanted me as much. People say beautiful things with blinks and unsaid thoughts. She said these things. Maybe I said a few of them too being so comfortable in my shoes as I was.

We fell into a back room, no one was there, or there was a few here and there. It seemed everyone was having sex. It was of normal fare.

Suddenly I thought of Leala. I was not married. Nor did I plan to be married. And really I thought to myself what is this small indiscretion in the way of life. Nothing. Unimportant really. That was so, I thought. That was all very true. But I still chose not to have sex with her that night. I lost my interest. As things sometimes happen this way. You understand.

I left her on a bed. Vulnerable in ways that mostly naked women are. She did not speak as I left. She did not have to. She moved quietly to another couple and joined.

The bed never looked more inviting than that moment. Empty now but the promise lingered. My hair felt thinner than before.
I went outside and had two smokes. Damn cheap cigarettes.

Damn Leala for buying such cheap cigarettes. However smoking two cigarettes allowed me to watch the sunrise. Such a beautiful thing to see. I let the second cigarette burn to filter.

Eventually I made it back to Richards's house. I found Leala sleeping. Naked in the arms of a man I did not know.

Tears came to my eyes. They collected at the bottom but did not fall. But I knew that it did not matter. Not in the way of life you know.

I found a small rock in my pocket, from where I do not know. I rubbed it between my thumb and finger. Perhaps I was waiting for a genie, or a sign. I must have been waiting for something. Leala did not wake up as I stood there. Rub. Rub. I decided to leave.

I walked outside and lit another smoke. I only had one now. Damn Leala. Damn her.

I stood there on the lawn. My feet not yet ready to leave I suppose. I had no reason to be on the lawn more than in my car. I just was not yet moving.

Standing there near the end of my cigarette I heard a bird chirp.

Then two or three more birds began chirping. My heart leapt. I returned into the house and woke Leala gently. I moved her hair with two fingers. Thick and beautiful. I whispered in her ear "I love you. Sweet Leala. My sweet Leala."

She only turned into the arms of her lover.

I placed the small rock next to her. I left then. I had no more cigarettes to smoke. Not even cheap ones.

The sun was fully up and the birds were chirping.

I speak of Truth and Love

"The stars are beautiful
Like your eyes-"

I continued to speak
Of fingernails and snails
Of wind and wishes
And love, always of love

"So what do you say,
About Agamemnon
And the Holy Ghost

Trees bleeding saffron
And love making on the moon?"

She looked at me as I spoke
Then with her red lips said
"I fucked your brother doggy style
And let him cum all over my face.

But I don't love him like I love you."

Truth and Love
So happy together

Calling the Ex

They were married after all
So it shouldn't have been such a shock
When I called and he answered out of breath
And she, the one I called for, was right there

Though not really there at all.
The embarrassment is mine
But not for calling,
No that really couldn't have been helped

I had no way of knowing.
My embarrassment
Came from remembering her
As mine.

Burning Dear John

I slept today
Or maybe it was yesterday
I don't know
Heartbeats ceased making sense of time

I scratched out a message to the gods
On another empty match book.
I am mailing it to NASA
To send to the heavens.

"I've been missing you since before I knew you were"
She smiled
She said she felt the same way once,
About tea and cigarettes.

"Did I see you? On the stairs?"
I breathed, hoping she would catch it.
Hoping she would before leaving
For the moon.

Gravity

Where was I
When gravity came calling?

Just finishing breakfast
Still safely wrapped
In my own brand of daily depression
- get up, go to work, go home, go to bed –
I was only on step two of this process

How can I forget?

The silence, the noise
The calm, the confusion
The paradox completing the squared circle
In my own personal
Ground zero

Where was I
When the mass of it all
Seemed to instantly double
And the world came tumbling down?

I was in Baltimore,
New York,

Pennsylvania

And D.C.

I was with everyone
And I was alone.

To Tyus

Everytime we say goodbye
it seems to get harder for me
and easier for you

Even if I moved next door
or in the same house
I can see that you are going to go
your own way

And do things that don't include
falling asleep in my arms
holding my hand
or asking me to get something
because it is just to high

All I can do
to delay inevitable
is squeeze you tighter
hold you longer
take pictures of you sleeping

And store away
a million million
memories

I miss you

Vicious sewing machine

I have typed, deleted, typed again. This is one of those things. Something I am dying to say and I am afraid I can't say it correctly. I am thinking of saying nothing. I am afraid I will say too much.

I think I am hoping to find things here that I lack in the corporeal world. Yes. That is sad. And dumb. I have no real hope of such things. It is like there are two of me. Perhaps there are more. Anyway, I am sorry for this. Even before it really begins I am sorry. I am sorry there are too many. That this is too long. And that it is too much like other ones.

And this is not helping. This is more like stalling. This is more like speaking of the weather. Speaking of anything but 'this.'

I certainly felt closer to saying it a minute ago. I paused. It didn't really pass but it feels buried. I am good like that.

I am going to puke.

It is like this now at 26. Knowing what it is like to be alone. I don't think of you anymore. Maybe because I force myself not to. Maybe because I have nothing left to think about. It is stale. Like the air in my bedroom. Like the feeling of my sheets. It is stale. Pictures of my kids still sit in a box. Next to the dresser. Why am I afraid of them?

I vacuumed and opened all the windows. I left for two days. And when I came home I day dreamed. I heard noises. It sounded like laughter. I opened my refrigerator. The grapes were old. I ordered a pizza and a 2-liter of coke.

I can't make it real. The refrigerator is too loud. The lights too strong. The cars break my day. I don't hear laughter.

My TV isn't on. I try to make out my face in the black screen. Maybe years went by.

Does your hand feel like I imagine? Would you release a small smile if I bit your ear?

I put a chair on my balcony. I can't see any stars. Light pollution. I pretend the planes are aliens coming to take me away.

They never stop to beam me up.

I start laundry. It finishes. I put it away. I am older now.

I check my answering machine.

I record new greetings. I stop at sunrise.

The thought of somebody calling and hearing my new hilarious greeting fills me with joy.

I laugh. And laugh. Until I cry. Nobody calls.

I lay down on the kitchen floor. Listening for footsteps. Are you barefoot? My finger traces the outline of your imagined footprint. I think we are happy.

It's Monday. Or Tuesday. Maybe Wednesdaythursdayfriday. Weekend. Week begin. 10 years go by. My floor needs cleaning.

I return to my room. My bed. My sheets.

The air is stale. But I'm used to it.

Really.

This is the title

I am a lonely, sad, bastard. This much is true. I waste my days spending time thinking about how lonely I am, how sad I might be, and how much of a bastard I can become. In this way I feel close to God. I think God is lonely. I think God is sad because like me he is lonely. I think many people forget about God, or think that God, because of his talents or looks or whatever doesn't mind being God. But I think there are days that God just has had enough of being God and wants to be a bastard to people. He, like me, has dreams.

I had a conversation with God the other night when Wendy played head games with me. I still hope that was just a scare tactic of some sort. Or me and God will have more conversations.

Anyway, like I was saying. I had a conversation with God. It went more or less like this, "God, if you are real, and not just some form of reassurance that my culture has thought up, then please help me out. Why you should do this, I cannot say nor do I feel I should. You are God, you should know why or why you should not. I am wondering now, if you are really just a part of me, a part of my subconscious, or my otherness that I can talk to. I can blame bad things on you or blame them on me but who cares bad things happen either way. This conversation has suddenly lost meaning. You are not doing well here God. I need some sort of support and you are silent. This silent act is really dumb. Fuck it. Save me. Die of cancer. I don't care. Right now, I just don't want this kid."

That is more or less my conversation. It didn't go that well. Or it went really well. I haven't really decided on how I feel about it. It doesn't really matter. I am in this not really mattering kind of mood. It goes along with my personality that I am wearing right now. Is it the lack of love?

I was out and about, or whenever I am out and about I look at people. I see them. I see them with other people. I see them holding hands. I see them kissing. I see them feeling things for each other. I see this and I am disgusted.

Really I am.

At me. Mostly just at me. I am disgusted at myself for not having that. But I am a saboteur. I do not keep relationships very long, I end them. I find reasons. I create reasons. I am the reason. Nothing is perfect. Find me. Help me. Fuck off.

I see so many beautiful people. Men. Women. Together. Alone, but not alone like I am alone. I see that sometimes too. I see alone people like me, alone. You can see that aloneness, you can feel that aloneness. You have all seen it, or felt that aloneness from someone. It is pathetic. It is scary. It is uncomfortable to be near. It is so desperate in its need that it drives away the very thing it is looking for. I am embarrassed of my on aloneness, and this drives me to more aloneness. I am sick. I am sick. I am sick, and I am so beautiful because of it.

Not really, but I think that helps me make it through. Who needs drugs when I have my own head to get me high, to get me low, to get me what I need when I need it. Fuck me. I say that to myself. I am my best friend and I hate myself.

I am sick like a teenager is sick with this bullshit. I think maybe I have not grown up. I think maybe I am holding on to things I need not hold on to. I think maybe I am still waiting for that bus. You know that bus that I am waiting for right? Isn't this the fucking bus stop? Help me. Save me. Fuck off.

I am pushing and I am pulling. I am being here and I am feeling there. I can be next to you, please let me be next to you. I am needy in my neediness. Can you deal with that? I can be there for you; I can do things to you. I can play these sweet fucked up games or we can just watch TV and masturbate next to each other. I don't care. I just need your skin, your breath, your hair, your scent, your liquid self next to mine. I am waiting...

If someone is still listening that is fine. That is fine. That is fine. Somewhere I have left clues to which I am somewhere I have given you bad directions. Because I am still waiting...

I can recognize things in myself in others. I can see what it is that I think it is that I see. I know what I mean, and they know what I mean, and they are out there and they can see what it is that I think that I see and I think that maybe we know what it is and why it is but we are not going to say it here. Not with the rest of you all listening in to our secret conversation. Isn't that right? Tell me that is right, tell me in that way we speak to each other in that way we seek each other out in that way..oh shit..oh fuck...I am alone and no one hears me, no one feels this right here, fuck me fuck me fuck me...

So much of the outside world, I mean outside of my own head, tells me I am so beautiful, tells me my face is so beautiful, tells me my eyes are so beautiful, tells me my words are so beautiful, tells me I am so beautiful, so beautiful, so beautiful, so beautiful I have grown numb to world and all her fractions, all her stretching of beings. My beautifulness has grown on me like a cancer and has eaten me whole, how beautiful is that? FUCK YOU. Save me. Help me.

I have heard things. I have heard things. I have heard things.

I wonder what it is that I am after. I wonder what it is that I want. I wonder if I find it what I will do with it. I wonder if it is real. I wonder if it is defined. I wonder who the fuck I am. I wonder why you listen to me. I wonder why I speak. I wonder what it is that I want. I wonder if you are it. I wonder if you are there. I wonder if you are you. I wonder if you know you are the you I want, I need, I cry for, I beg for. I am shameless and disgusting. I am beautiful in my rise and fall. Watch me TURN AWAY AND FUCK OFF. Please stay and help me light this fucking town up. I am going to explode like a muthafucking a-bomb. I'm going to take this world by the balls and when I reach the top, I going to stand there like I always knew this is my role. I am the king of this place. I am the king. Watch me as I take the stage. I was born to rock; I was born to be worshiped. I was born wear the crown

Eh.

Bla

Fuck off

Stop reading

Fuck you

I didn't mean it

Come here

Kiss me

Love me

Bite my lip

Make me bleed

make me believe

in you

in us.

in

,. l;mfdsal;fdsa

fdsa
fdsa

fds

(me)

here i come

sometimes i just want to be missed. by someone. for something. for anything. it can be mutual. but mostly it is a solo affair. being missed means being gone. i do that well. do you do it well? maybe we could do it together. be gone. be missed. missing.

i'm not so pretty. i'm not so tall. i'm not so whatever it was i dreamed of. but i still want to be. i'm still young. my hair is going grey. my hair is getting thinner. my gut is getting bigger. my memories more profound. the world is growing complicated. and i just want the simplicity of yesteryear. one thousand sunday sunday's and i miss. one thousand thousand still to come and i still dream.

watch me fly once. it will be grand. just wait. just wait for it to come. i'm telling you. it will be something.

and i'll wait for you. and we'll wait. under the same stars. under it all. where it doesn't really matter anymore. but we'll still fly anyway right? just to show 'em. just to show 'em we can do it. be missed. be missing. flying. dying. look at me. look away. here i come. just wait.

i feel small some days. i feel yeah. i feel that.

sometimes in the tub. when the water is getting cold. and my hand isn't holding the glass upright any longer. i remember what it was. i remember how it was. yeah i remember that.

no tears baby baby. no tears tonight.
hmmmmmmm hmmmmmmmm hmmmmmmm

exhale baby.

i'll fly one day. and it will be grand. you just wait.

yeah you wait. you'll see.

Mt. Vernon

Because you've seen TV

I am really unable to begin this in any sort of artistic way. I have no talent for that. I have been feeling like I have things to say but no way really to express them. Perhaps I have had no real decent time. I feel at the moment this could be the time, I also feel rather bland right now. Rather forcing the issue instead of letting it the issue force me. It is this way, or really, it has been this way for quite some time. I cannot seem to find the time to find the right keystrokes that open the flood gates and lets you all know or really more interesting to me, lets me know exactly or at least in some sort of small way what it is that I am feeling and thinking and hoping. I use writing as a release. It is a means not an end for me. My purpose is beyond the writing, beyond the words it is in the message or behind the message or around the message or maybe just ahead of the message. I am never sure where or what it is but I know there is something there or at least I mean to say I feel like there is something there. This is what I do. Or why I write. To find out what it is that I am doing.

Earlier today I felt more passionate than I do right now. I felt more -- there. I cannot apologize for this. It is and there isn't much more I can do about it. I am only hoping my typing more and more that it will find its way out and find its way here. Find its way to my screen.

I am busy keeping secrets from myself. I am busy being frustrated at my own inability to let me in. There is an honesty I keep on the shelf. It is like fine wine. The taste, even the smell, is unmistakable and draws you in. I can see my bottle but I cannot reach her. I cannot touch her. She is out of reach. She is out of me. What am I? Why should I care about it? It is only a bottle. She was only here for a spell.

I have begun the move. 21236 is the zip code. Come find me. I am here. I am here and I have nothing to tempt you with. I have nothing to save you with. I have everything that somebody thinks is gold and somebody else thinks is trash and I am confused and hurt and spiteful and full of something that I want to give you. It is me, really, but it isn't me. It is me that moves like water. My strength is mysterious like wind. I have this to give I have it to give because it burns to hot for me to hold. It is a book with my signature on the cover and a stain from my tongue on the spine. Take it away from me. Come take me away. Take me away. Take me. Away.

Sometimes I think I can struggle forever.

I want you to think I am beautiful but only after you see how ugly I really am. I want you to think how spectacular my light is only after you see that it isn't that bright, that strong, that big and it certainly won't last. I have limitations and I want you to think I am all the more beautiful for it.

I am a master mason that can construct a great many things of a near pure genius design and function. I know this because I know that I have constructed my many failures and my many successes and I have done it while not looking while not seeing while not understanding that I had this power. I have a temple and a god. I made them last night out of dreams and wishes. They are so strong as to stand up to all kinds of torture and pain and failure and disappointment. They can even stare reality in his ugly stupid face. I spit. I laugh. I scream in the face of reality.

My temple, my god is so strong she can do all of these things. Only life can stop me.

There is plenty of hope out there. Just none for us.

I heard that today. I read it actually. I read it and wept. Inside of course. Inside. It is always on the inside. Yet this isn't why I came here today. No this is just a dance. A song. A play. A invitation to my bed.

Sometimes my feet get cold and sometimes I would do anything just to see her again.

you sit there with your blanket of mysterious and truths with your bottle of friends and plate lies and you tell me things you believe because you've seen tv and you think your so smart and your so strong and your so cunning and so clever and so with it and so on top of it all but you don't know me you don't know yourself your naked feet stink of uncertainty and you breath crawls across the air on its belly because despite your righteous attitude your breath knows, oh it knows it lacks the credentials to walk to my ear. your sing song moon does little to my eyes does little for my belly does little for my future my past my now. your

kings and queens and love of tarot and all things unknown does not paint my sky with pinks and purples and greens and happy little children. you know nothing you say nothing you pretend nothing you claim nothing you live for nothing you die for nothing you are in the end nothing and all your bottles and all your blankets and all your noise will be swept away in one powerful stroke from life's unyielding hand. do not ever sit up higher than the lowest of the insects that crawl around eating the food that has fallen from your open mouth the mucus that fallen from your bleeding nose the small bits of shit that have shaken lose from the hairs of your ass crack. this insect is royalty compared to you and your thoughts your constructed thoughts of genius and specialness and uniqueness and wonderfulness and all this thought of woman and man and laugh and spirit in what is nothing but rock. oh i can feel what cannot be felt i can hear what cannot be said and i can see what cannot be described yes yes yes you silly fuck you silly dim witted fuck you better worship that bug that insect as your master. watch him as he crawls so focused on his life so unconcerned with your shoe with your dreams
your wishes what of him! what of his life you split apart with your weight, your fatness your pathetic

fatness of mind of thought watch this bug do his work without complaint without hope without love without need of more than what he can find on his own. there is no moon singing to the cockroach. there is no sea maiden for ant. there is no need for a heaven to make things right for beetle or maggot. there is no one to care and they are fine with that. you stupid fuck. you are so smart in your ways in your so fantastic ways you can't even get out of your own misery your own dreams choke you. and you die. you die alone. you die with hope. you die with the moon singing to you. la dee da la dee da la dee da. you die and the maggots eat you and the cockroaches fuck in your once fat belly and the beetles shit in your once beautiful hair and crawl on over to your once so wonderful high minded soul. what was your mother's mother's mother's mother's mother's mother's mother's mother's mother's mother's mother's name? you don't know you don't know where is her soul her mind her hopes her dreams her fears do you care do you wonder do you think do you believe you are so special that they will remember you? you! you are so unique in this world? the bugs are calling you. these unique maggots are wanting to swap soul stories. he's got the whole world in his hand. he is bacteria. virus. fire. ending. beginning. he is a program. you are a line of code. not even that. part of a line of code. a character in a long program. you will be quickly forgotten. thank you for your time. the insects thank you for yet another meal. thank you for having children. the insects need to eat in the future. thank you. now shut up.

it is a cold rainy day here in baltimore. i would like company.

Baltimore Nights

I want to hear them through the walls.

I want to be closer to them having sex. Not because I am sick but because I miss love.

Sometimes I pick up the phone and dial. Pause. Breathe. And hang up again.

I don't think we speak the same language anymore And I am afraid to find out if it's true.

I want to let you in but I don't want to be easy or cheap.

I want it to be like the orchard summer of '84. Hell I would even take another Honolulu of '99 when we whispered to our friends and parents about lost selves and borrowed time.

I would like to borrow some more time. Maybe to squeeze your hand. Pass a note. Say I'm sorry.

Maybe we could change the stars. Or the wind. Or lift the fog.

In dreams.

In Baltimore.

Splish Splosh

I am just going to sit here and type. I am bored. My head hurts. I am kind of tired. I just put on Jack Johnson. I want to go home. I sort of want company. But not new company. I don't want to entertain. I just want to hang out. I want old company. But I don't have any old company that I want to hang out with. I just want to relax. Watch a movie. Listen to music. Say a little. Say a lot. Drift away. Hold a hand. I certainly don't have a hand to hold. I like to squeeze thumbnails. Not hard. Just enough. I am dumb like that. Why does any of this matter? I suppose it doesn't really. I am bored. What can I say? I am feeling rather like this. Rather like wanting to not be alone. Rather like wanting. I want a lot maybe. I don't know. I don't much of anything at the moment. I am tired. More tired than I was a few minutes ago. Yadda yadda yadda yadda. I wrote an email to a stranger. She responded. It was okay. It wasn't bad. It was short. I felt rather cheated. I didn't write a short email. I got a short email in return. Is it really about giving? I am not so sure. I don't think I'm selfish.
Maybe I compare too much. Maybe I should care less. Maybe I should be more like how I pretend to

be sometimes. Maybe I should just shut up. I probably sound like a little baby. You know sometimes I really do want to cry. Sometimes I do. Sometimes I do right here and you probably don't notice. You probably couldn't notice. I never really say anything about it. What am I to say? I cried today? Well, who cares? Who are we to each other anyway? Voices at most. Text most of the time. I am text as this is as real as I am most times. Sad. That is what I think about it sometimes. Quite sad. This is as real as I am most times and here in text you can't hear me. I can't hear you. I can't get you a drink. You can't fast-forward past the previews on the rented movie. Or maybe we got a DVD. Maybe we cut directly to your favorite part. Maybe you want to share something with me. Maybe a bit of knowledge maybe a secret maybe just something you thought. And I could smile. And I can see how much of a fool I really am. Opinions are more than like assholes. They are a part of us. A deeper part of us than maybe we can admit. Or am I just being really stupid right here. Yeah. Who knows? Maybe you have an opinion on the matter. Maybe you want to say "what is the matter?" Maybe I could tell you. Maybe I could say it. Probably not. I don't know. Who am I? To say this or that or anything at all. Just save me once. Just once. I need to be saved then I could save you 1,000 times. One for 1,000 what a deal. You can do it right? NO. NO. I didn't really think so. I really didn't believe it could be true. But I dreamed about it. I really did. I still do. On most nights actually. Most nights I dream of being that way again. I don't want to. Or at least part of me doesn't want to. Fuck emails. Fuck writing long emails to strangers. I don't want a stranger really. I don't want new company. Get it? Anybody feelin' this right here? I wish I was smarter than I am. Or dumber. Or just different. We all want to be different. We are all the same like that. I want this. I want that. I want something that I cannot define. I don't car about your car. Your house. Your kite. Your dog. Your brand new shoes. I want something more than what can be touched, bought, traded, or something else like that. I don't know. What the fuck do I know? I have grown some over the course of time. Who are some of you out there? I think I am too disgusting for some people to read on any sort of regular basis. This doesn't bother me that much. It does at some level. I want to be well thought of. Who doesn't really. At some level. YA YA YA YA YA YHA YHA YAYAYAYAYAYa. I should just go on some dumb ass show like Oprah. Talk about it. About what? About this. About that. What does it matter? Can you see I am confused? Can you see I don't know anything at all? Isn't it there, in the stars? I don't need you. I know that. I need me. I need me to be something. To be me I suppose. I am great company. I keep my company all the time. I make myself laugh. Fuck the rest. Or not. Maybe they could laugh too. I don't know. Who knows? It never works out. There is always something in the way. Mostly me I guess. This way. That way. Yaddda yadda yadda. I've been writing what nonstop for 15 minutes and I am no closer to a point than I was when I started. This is dumb. This is stupid. I don't really mean it, but I do enough where it hurts a bit. Am I crazy? I don't think so. I think maybe if anything I am honest. If anything I am there. Right there listening or trying to figure it all out and I am telling you about it. Whoever you are? I don't know. I don't want to pretend I know. I can't. I could maybe. I want to change skin right now. I want to change something. Something important, something.....

one day i'll find the way to speak clearly. and when i do. maybe somebody can see me. maybe then i could be heard. maybe then. maybe then....

Charles Street Romance

I am tired of trying to be clever, I just want to tell you the damn story the way I remember it. It's about space and timing although some of you will think it is about a man and a woman. I guess it is about that too, but mostly it is about space and timing.

It doesn't start the way great stories start. It wasn't raining and I don't think it was that cold outside either. I didn't have my poncho or my umbrella. I just had me. I was wearing flip flops one size too large. Blue and worn, I don't think anybody ever noticed they were just a bit too big for me. My jeans were ripped near my heel from dragging on the ground and my shirt was beginning to fade from too many washings. I didn't think about meeting her that night but like I said, this story is about timing.

And space.

She wasn't that overly beautiful girl that you might be thinking about. Yeah, she was a blonde but sometimes it seems like all of them are these days. She had blue eyes and yeah, they were something to look at but you wouldn't stop breathing if she looked at you or anything. I liked the way she dressed, in jeans and some button up shirt of some sort that said "I'm from California" even though she was only from some town outside of Baltimore. For whatever reason it didn't seem fake on her, she wasn't trying to be what she was, she was just being it. You have no idea how attractive that was to me at that moment. How many times do we meet people who just slither around in their own skin trying so hard to project some fantasy image they have of themselves on to you. As if you care. As if you would give a damn that they really can't afford that watch or that those shoes. I don't know maybe it's just me. Maybe it's because I wear flip flops from Wal-Mart that are one size too big.

So we started talking. How that came to be isn't so important. We started talking about politics and life and she had opinions. Not your everyday opinions like "I don't like Bush because the economy sucks" or "Republicans are liars." No, she had real reasons for her opinions, like something about the quality of the people Bush was selecting to be Justices and she rattled off some startling information about the problems of some of these candidates. It wasn't in that huffy puff way that some people do things. You know that way when people know something they get loud and excited and slam down the information upon your ears with triumphant arm waving. She did none of that and suddenly I became enchanted by the movement of her lips.

Nice and full formed they moved comfortably on her face. Sometimes I have noticed women speak quickly as if speaking were a crime or that their lips can only be perfect in the position they were in when the final bit of lip gloss was applied. She had such a beautiful slight smile that seduced me a good two feet away. What would they be like to bite? What if it was raining and I had an umbrella to protect her? I should have shaved.

Suddenly she had to go so I grabbed a napkin and wrote: "Kristin's fake number is:"

She smiled and stared at the napkin for a few moments. I think it was a new form of murder she was trying out. I said something like help but it came out as "Come on. A fake number, how hard could it be?"

She gave me a number.

Could this be some story I tell my children?

I called her and we went out. It wasn't a fake number and I wore real shoes.

I picked her up and she seemed a bit nervous but not overly.

"Have you been married?"

Yes, I said. More aware of how small my Civic is.

"Do you have kids?"

Yes, two. Wrong turn. Where am I going?

Don't look so upset I said. Please don't look upset I thought. Wouldn't a fake number feel better now? I wished it were snowing but it was too early for that.

Everything felt built up like a house of cards and as long as nobody touched it or no wind blows it might as well be a castle made of stone. We went out another night after that and then made plans for a Saturday. Then she said she couldn't see me. I said maybe some other time and she said sure. Some other time.

She called me later that same Saturday. She drove to a bar she had never been to. We kissed. She has beautiful lips. I played with her fingers between mine. We stood in silence and I didn't know who I was anymore. I called her. She was busy.

I called her. She was busy.

I called her. She was busy.

I never saw or heard from her again.

boy

i'm still that boy you've always known
still swaying where the screen door should be
still holding my tin cup singing something sad
something unintelligible
but unmistakably sad

if only i didn't jump
if only i didn't stutter
if only i didn't shut up
if only i didn't whatever
then
you know

maybe it would have made a difference
maybe napoleon would have won
maybe anastasia would have outrun the commies

and we would have had our shot
to fall in, to fall out
do what lovers do
at midnight and during bankers hours
in grass fields and empty stadiums
where people are or were
once staring at the stars

it could have been great
it could have been grand

but it's like that dog you've never met
or that story you didn't hear

it's little and unimportant
but to some
maybe to a boy in baltimore

it could have changed the world

lover

sometimes i try so hard. i try so hard to be poetic. to be heard. to be different. and it doesn't matter.

maybe i'm no different than you. maybe i can't stand you because i am just like you. and i can't stand me. not right now anyway.

i think i really could be. somebody's

i'm not lying to you right now. i'm not pretending to say things just to say things. i am too humble for any of that.

it's not really like screaming into pillows. turning off the lights. closing the doors. eating ice cream at 2 am.

it's not really like seeing you coming off the plane. getting out of the shower. catching you staring off into space.

read this to me.

i can be somebody's

hey love,

sometimes i think i get more credit than i should. if you don't speak to me. how can i know or even possibly begin to see that i might be too dumb to notice? you have to open up more, risk more, strain for more to get closer to what is going on. why not speak to me? what would you lose? what do you think you have between us that you would lose? is gaining something here, now, between me and you not worth risking something? what keeps you from being honest? what is it that is so special that you won't be here now?

i am not a brilliant man. i shouldn't be treated as such. sometimes i don't know what i am talking about. listen to me or don't listen to me. but whatever you do. don't do it halfway. or no, do it halfway. what does it matter to me? i can't possibly ever know what it is i can't see if you never show it. i lose nothing. i lose something. it is all true. it is all bullshit. it is what we make it. somehow i don't think i am coming through to you in ways that i think i should. or want to. this is what it means. to say i know it doesn't matter when i tell you these things . you'll hear what you you'll hear in the end. you'll risk what you want to risk in the end. you'll put up with me as long as you want to.

i am pushing. i am pulling. i am yelling. i am screaming. i am hiding. i am doing what i can to make you see my shadow more than my skin. i want you to understand the contrast. or tell me it doesn't matter and mean it fully.

lies and truth. truth and lies. bugs and humans. who makes us so holy, so above it all? question me? doubt my sincerity? that is the way isn't it. i can be who i want to. and you'll still see me in frames. i am not afraid of that anymore. push me. i dare you. i want you to try and push me without pushing yourself. push me without doubting yourself. push me without ever wondering why. kiss my ear. take your coin. we will be closer than lovers. and know nothing of each other.

i watched a raven dance this morning.

baltimore.

is it real? to you? to me? can you guess? can you speak? can you understand? and if you do? how much does it mean? to you? to me? to them? to anyone?

oh - it matters. but not to royalty. not to the holy. are we all afraid of losing our place in the clouds?

are we afraid to not seem real?

i started

i started to say "i miss you."

remember back when promises meant something and stars seemed really bright and holding hands made butterflies? remember talking about the future and dreams and plans and hope? why didn't we ever discuss forgiveness? regret wasn't on the calendar. pain was myth. and love? half smiles always looked beautiful to me.

there is a reason we all have the names we do. there is a reason why we talked long after the dark. there is a reason why.

i started to say "i miss you."

it's never so easy to say 'hello' as it is the first time. but isn't it scary? isn't it just a little bit frightening to start? i've never been as strong as i was and i've never been so dumb since.

maybe we'll change. one by one. day by day. maybe we'll make a new path to new glory. but we have to start again don't we? we have to be there?

we have to say things we never thought about saying. open up. be vulnerable. be strong. be dumb. be again.

i started to say "i miss you."

i started to say it. i started to mean it. i started.

seeing the stars again. making promises in the dark. believing in them. believing in me. and growing more comfortable. with myself. with this life. with this. but it's so hard. being here. clutching leaves. breaking silence. breathing. being. alone.

the only one to know

this world tires me. if i were somebody else, one of you perhaps, i would explain this in some meaningful terms. create hyperlinks from my life to yours. merge my frustration with your understanding. instead i am reduced to this. stupid clever lines spilling across my screen. stupid clever lines that maybe i will repeat, or maybe you will. perhaps we will repeat them to each other. some strange human stereo of frustration and understanding. better than sex.

i can't relate to my present self. i am a foreigner to me. i am in a dangerous place. i'm in some mental state that isn't quite normal to my past or maybe it is and i've just simply forgotten how i normally am. i think i would hate myself if given the chance to meet me in some other place. far from here of course. far from here.

i am stuck in repetition. i am stuck. or maybe i just like it here. i can't tell anymore. i can't tell. i can't tell what it is that i want anymore.

i'm leaving you.

i want you to know that it's me and not you. it's me and not you. it's me and not you.

this is a mental murder. i'm turning myself in. i'm killing my name. i'm killing my name. i'm killing every fucking thing. and this isn't something you can relate to because for just once in my life i want to be the only one to know.

yeah, i'm selfish and stupid like that. couldn't you tell? didn't you notice?

nothing separates me from you. not religion, culture, history, time zones, area codes, sexual orientation, or sexual frequency. every rope you hang yourself with i've already dangled from or will soon. you've got your particulars. your husband. your drug abuse. your suicide attempts. your loneliness. your depth of emotion that no one else can touch. oh yeah, you got it all baby. all to yourself. right? and i, oh no, i am the only one here too. don't relate to this shit. don't fucking tell me it's going to be okay. you go over there. you hang yourself. i'll cut my ankles off. i'll do what i do because of me and only me. only me.

i'm sick of that.

i'm sick of saying it. hearing it. living it. escaping it. creating it. destroying it. being it.

can't you be here? can't we hurt each other instead of ourselves? can't we do something to be somebody else? can't we pretend to be rich? sex underneath the freeway, death in the snow. let's be japanese. let's be anything but now. let's be anything but alive.

i'll send a postcard. from time to time. from paris or moscow. we'll be friends.

just like old times.

Letter dated 03.03.29

I am staring at tits on my computer screen. It is the closest to flesh I have come to in more days than I can remember. I wrote to my Congressman today. I wrote him because I am afraid I am losing my mind and I need help.

At the very least I need a friend. I told him to do something quick. Represent me because I cannot represent myself. Tell me where to go, how to be and how to think. I do not know what I am doing anymore and I am less sure.

Have you ever tasted your own tears? It is something I look forward to doing at 5 PM. My after dinner treat to myself. I sit here at this table, fork and spoon to the right knife to the left. My glass filled with water and my plate still hot with chicken or pasta. My hands reach out, palm to God, and I pray for forgiveness. I eat quickly and quietly spending an equal amount of time looking at each of my three empty chairs. I use a napkin to wipe my mouth when I am done eating. How was your day, how was work, how was the drive, how was school, how is Mr. Jones, how is that project going, how is mother, how is brother, how lovely is my desert?

I should look into salt free tears. I am worried about my cholesterol.

Cleaning is easy and pointless. I think if I left it messy I could see signs of life that I am so desperately missing now. I don't know what I can do. I hope my Congressman comes soon. I went out to do laundry today and nobody said hello but a few people did look at me. I was worried that I had become invisible. I was worried I had already died.

Who would pick up my mail?

I told my Congressman about that too. I wouldn't want the city or my apartment complex to become burdened with reading and throwing away all of my junk mail. I will miss the Penny Saver. I will miss reading the personals and pretending that I can be a match. A soul mate and a lover for someone out there.

Maybe this girl here, with her soft blue eyes and nice red lips. Maybe if she got to know me we could hit it off.

Who am I kidding? Really who? No, really who?

I mean seriously who the fuck am I?

Dear Congressman,

My name is J. Tyler Blue. I was born November 23, 1976 in Portsmouth Virginia. My mom told me I could be anything I wanted to be. I want to be alive. Please help me.

All of my love,
J. Tyler Blue

Forever

I am sucking down this cigarette as furiously as I can. For me, a random smoker it tingles the back of my throat and warms my lungs. How much tar did I just put in there? Not enough. Not nearly enough.

It isn't the fact that I think this woman is beautiful and obviously out of my league it is the fact that she is. If I died right here outside of this cafe right now I would have better luck of having a person I didn't know five minutes ago put his or her lips on mine in some feeble attempt to rescue me than I would trying to talk to perfect fucking strangers in some far flung hope of romance. I give up. I want another cigarette.

I can't smoke in the cafe. Fuck the cafe. Fuck the beautiful woman with the light blue dress that is nearly form fitting. Not in some hooker come fuck me way, but that goddamn elegant way that says "Hi, I'm college educated and I play tennis on the weekends" way. I didn't want to drink another chai anyway. I am sick with sweet things in my life. I am sick with pretending to fit in to be this or be that. I am sick with desperately trying to stay somewhat connected with fashion trends and hip places. And yet I cannot commit myself to hang out with fashion-retarded people with horrible breath and bad foot wear. I am stuck in some nether world alone.

What now? Should I travel to the art museum and look at more wonderful things, inspiring things and try to muster all of intelligence into seeing what the artist was seeing? Understanding Art Movements for me is studying the absurd and ridiculous. I saw a red square not centered on a white background. It had the title of something like "Peasant woman represented by red square." Oh. Is that what the fuck that was! I thought it was a goddamn bullshark represented by the red square. Nothing is beautiful and simple and easy to hold anymore. Fuck me. I am going to need a new pack. I think I am swallowing this shit.

You know I had this dream the other night. It was about you and me. Fucking fantastic shit right?

You don't think I dream about you but I do. First off you think I don't even notice you, or certainly wouldn't write about you but I do notice and I am writing about you. I understand you have a certain distrust for what I say to you and you have some feeling perhaps unsaid feeling that I don't like you or at least that I may not like you as much as you think you might like me. Of course that isn't true. I have a mysterious way of playing against intuition. I have done this my whole life. It is the way I pause when I speak and the way I construct my sentence and the way I look at you when you are not looking at me.

I am writing this all for you right now as I walk around the city. I will of course type it later. I want you to know what I think about you and about me and us and all that stuff. Listen I don't do a good job of this, so this will be all kind of confusing and vague I guess because I just don't want to be hurt.

I had a dream about you. It was maybe two nights ago. We haven't emailed or communicated in any other fashion in some time. I thought once we were having a good start at a great relationship but things have sort of slipped away. Maybe it was me, maybe it was just the way things were but you know...things have drifted. I am babbling. I am an idiot and I should have never started this, but I have made commitments now and I have to see them through. I want to be remembered as a man who lived with some convictions you know.

Listen I just come right out and say that the dream was kind of sexual in nature. But don't think it was just some sort of sex fantasy thing. It wasn't like that. I am not like that. Sure, I look at porn sometimes. God, what am I saying? I just mean to say it wasn't like just sex. It wasn't me and you and a hotel room.

It was laughing. There was laughing and man did that feel great. Do you know how long it has been since I have laughed with a woman? Sometimes during our instant messages I would laugh and I guess I really thought we could laugh together. I dreamed that you would tilt your head back sometimes and bring your right hand up towards your mouth. Maybe you are shy about your mouth, but you have a lovely smile. It was bright in my dream. We were light and moved like clouds. We were in a town then a park. Have you been to Alaska? I haven't but I dreamt we could be there with smiles and an umbrella. It rained but we only had one umbrella so we shared. I made sure you were covered but it was coming down hard and I just wanted to be close.

Your hair smelled wonderful. Your finger traced the scar on my left cheek. The rain kept coming and we lowered the umbrella in a movement that seemed to take days. I bit your bottom lip and you smiled. My lips traveled just barely missing your skin until I came to your ear. Now your mouth was near my ear and I felt you breathe. The warm air crashed into my ear and butterflies filled my stomach. Raindrops pelted us. My tongue deftly moved your ear lobe to my teeth. Your nails began to dig into my arms as you inhaled sharply. I smiled and let lose a small laugh and moved to see your eyes. Wild filled I wished to dominate you and your eyes spoke of a desire to be dominated. I grabbed your hair violently and my teeth meet the flesh of your neck your hands and nails tore into me.

What happened to our clothes I cannot say but we were there now on the ground with rain coming down on our naked bodies. You were lying on your back and my mouth moved to discover you. My left hand clenched your right hand tightly as my right hand moved to part your legs. First I passed over you with my lips separated and you felt my breath on you. My tongue then slowly came out and then back in, my lips touched yours and you tensed your body. Suddenly my tongue came out with a passionate rage and your body jerked. My arms were curled under your legs and my hands grabbed your upped thigh firmly. You were mine there.

That was my dream. It was only a dream but it was more than that. I think I wanted to have a connection with you. But I do not know how to say so, to do so. I am, you know, alone in this world. Despite the thousands of other lonely people who live probably just miles away from me it is you who I want to see and I don't know. I guess I am some kind of pathetic loser.

These cigarettes are not doing it fast enough for me. And now that I have confessed and squared myself to best of my ability with this place, I just don't think there is anything more for me to do. I am not for this world. I cannot bear to be alone anymore. I cannot bear the sadness of waking up after dreams where I am not alone. I will not suffer anymore. I have enough GHB to end this.

I will dream of you forever now. I hope you live a happy life.

Nothing

I have nothing to say. I suppose I am letting you know that now in case I say something later and you happen to stop reading before that moment, just know it was nothing.

I am not eating as much. I am not writing as much. Maybe they are connected. I ate today, I am writing now. Life is a cherry or something else, something stupid. Eat toes. I am not up on politics like other people. I have a boring job so I won't talk about it. I don't date so there is nothing to say about that. I don't have friends. I do I suppose but not really close ones. There is nothing to report on these people. My kids are fine. Hooray. I don't take pictures so don't look for them. I have been dreaming lately. At night, in the morning mostly between alarms. During the 'snooze' time. Some during the day.

My mind feels diseased. I feel diseased. I say this to myself for my records. Maybe this can be read by someone, maybe me and I can say yes I was diseased then, but I am better now. The fall is coming. Then winter, then spring, then summer.

Another year will pass. And I wonder how much more will I go on like this, how much more will I?

Some days ago I was at Barnes and Noble. They have a Starbucks there and I sat down near the window with my Henry Miller book and I was reading it and eating some sandwich I ordered there with an iced chai. I was reading and sometimes I would stop and look out the window. What I was doing, yes, what I was doing was looking out the window and reading in-between but I would like to say and think it was the other way. But it was not.

I was looking for you

I was hoping I would see you

I was hoping, yes, waiting, for you to recognize me there in the window and you could come in and sit next to me and we could talk. We could share laughs and we could skip down the street and we could do whatever we wanted to do. Yes, I was waiting for you. But you did not come. And I ate alone, and drank my chai and read my book and watched the people go by.

There were so many people, young and old. And fat many people were fat and I thought if I would end up that way fat and alone one-day in the window of Barnes and Noble will that be me? Will I be there then waiting for you and what would you wear when I am old and fat? I do not want to think about it. It is a terrible depressing thing to think about.

I saw some women walking. Beautiful women and I began to see that I really love women, all sorts of women and I can see that these women or most of them anyway are sad. They are not lonely like me and they do not see me because I am there in the window to be seen so naturally they do not see me. I am you see something ugly and terrible. I am alone and nobody wants that. But...I see them...and they are horribly sad.

They are sad because their life lacks substance and I can see this in the way the walk and how they talk to each other. Their eyes dart around looking, looking, looking for life. The ones with men, yes, these ugly men with their dumb tennis shoes and their beer bellies and tank tops and baseball caps they do not know that their woman next to them is dying. And I think, and I know I could save them. In them I could rescue their lives.

I am, you must understand, a starving man who can see. I have eaten well, I was raised with the talent and means of a fine life but now I have fallen on difficult times and I am starving. And I see these women, these women are beautiful things to be eaten and enjoyed and they are dying with this man of theirs and they know it. They know that their gift and their talent is being wasted on Thursday nights in fifteen minutes of pumping and a few moans and a few groans and it is now 12:00 and TV and fart and sleep. Slobs of men. This fruit in their face and they turn their fat bellies, their ruddy cheeks, their small cocks, their bad teeth to the side. Get me a beer honey. Hey let us go out to the bar. Let us die a little slower tonight honey. That is what these slobs of men say but they do not even know it.

And these women settle for it because they are scared to be alone, like me. So instead they are sad. And they are dying. And they are wasted.

One night and we could both be born again. One night, this is what I dream, one night with one woman and we could both be resurrected from our early graves. What is more delicious than a woman? What is more ready than a man who dreams of such things? I would savor this; I would not bully my way through like some brute drunk off of whiskey. No! My nose my mouth my breath my tongue need to bask in these moments. Soak them up and slowly I would peel away the inhibitions of you. Your hips are nice to bite. Does he bite them? No! He is a fool. He only does what? ABC on your velvet! What amateur. What nonsense. What pathetic skill.

I would make you beg for my tongue inside of you. I would make you beg for my fingers to insert themselves and they would. And still I would bite your hips. And still I would grab your hand and still I would not let you go. No. You must wait. You must be reborn and rebirth is not given so easily.

And so I would treasure you. Your treasure and I would become intimate and lovers. And your body and mine would glide. And CLAW and GRAB and RIP and FIGHT and BURN and PULL and TEAR and FEEL

Yes we would feel –feel- feel what it is be alive. And this is not over at midnight and this is not TV and this is not Thursday night and we would wake the neighbors the kids the dogs the small animals outside! They would all disappear to us and we would appear to them.

I am in you. And we fight to stay together and to break apart because it is just too much. My skin is not enough to hold me. And you begin to tear it off of me and I begin to eat you out of your flesh and we leave this world. We leave it behind

What moves do we do? What positions and such things? We do not think of them. We do not even remember them in this fury. Who can remember birth?

Who can remember becoming alive?

Like we would be.

And this is why I am late to work everyday. And this is why I hit snooze. And this is why I wait for you at bookstores. And this is why I write nothing. And this is how you have diseased my mind. And this is me still waiting…

From the Author

Most of these are done in the third person but I wanted to take a moment and write to you, the reader, from me, the author. I don't want to get into my boring history too much but I think it is always a bit interesting to know where people come from and a little bit about who they are. I grew up all over the United States for various reasons I won't get into here. I've lived in nine states and also Japan. I have only truly loved one woman and by her I have two wonderful children. She is now married to some other guy and lives in Ohio. Most of these stories and poems are at least based in fact. Read them and you can conjure up some image of me. Of course, like you, the whole of me cannot be contained in one small book such as this. I hope though that in reading this book some small part of me was able to connect with some small part of you. In this connection I hope we can both come away feeling a little bit more human and a little bit more alive. Thank you for taking the time to read this and thanks for buying it, or stealing it, or whatever you did to get your hands on it. Hopefully we can meet up again some day.

J. Tyler Blue

www.jtylerblue.com

PretendGeniusPress

Our chief prostitute, the national award winning ad writing editor on vacation this month, once confided to Idi Amin, "I'm tired. If you ever decide to get out of politics there's always a place for you with me in Editing." Reportedly, Mr. Amin winced and gestured toward the horizon. It wasn't long thereafter that the unreported deaths of the underground writers who published_writeThis.com finally surfaced. Now beginning their second year of obscurity, these awardless amnesiacs have emerged looking pale and out of time sequence. You, the good people of Literachoo, have the opportunity to be remembered as the original donors of these once wretched intoners.

For a complete catalog of other fine publications by pGpr visit
www.pretendgenius.com

www.ingramcontent.com/pod-product-compliance
Ingram Content Group UK Ltd.
Pitfield, Milton Keynes, MK11 3LW, UK
UKHW041411180426
11947UKWH00007B/63